LEARN TO READ

LAURA LEE
and the
Little Pine Tree

by Alice Sullivan Finlay
illustrated by Julie Durrell

ZondervanPublishingHouse
Grand Rapids, Michigan

A Division of HarperCollinsPublishers

Laura Lee and the Little Pine Tree
Text copyright © 1993 by Alice Sullivan Finlay
Illustration copyright © 1993 by Julie Durrell

Requests for information should be addressed to:
Zondervan Publishing House
Grand Rapids, Michigan 49530

Library of Congress Cataloging-in-Publication Data

Finlay, Alice Sullivan.
    Laura Lee and the little pine tree / Alice Sullivan Finlay.
        p. cm.
    Summary: While spending the weekend in a mountain cabin worrying about a number of things, Laura Lee learns to apply the Bible verse, "If you have faith as a mustard seed . . . Nothing will be impossible for you."
    ISBN 0-310-59861-3 (pbk.)
    [1. Mountain life—Fiction. 2. Worry—Fiction. 3. Christian life—Fiction.] I. Title.
PZ7.F49579Las   1993
[E]–dc20   93-7429
                                                            CIP
                                                            AC

Edited by Dave Lambert and Leslie Kimmelman
Interior and cover design by Steven M. Scott
Illustrations by Julie Durrell

Printed in the United States of America

96 97 98 / CH / 10 9 8 7 6 5 4 3 2

For my husband, Richard,
and our mountain getaways.

CHAPTER ONE

Laura Lee sniffed
the fresh mountain air.
A red cardinal jumped
onto a little pine tree.
"Is that our cabin?"
asked Laura Lee.

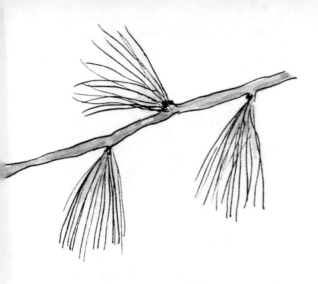

"That is it," said Dad.

"This is great!" said Randy.

The last few red maple leaves
fell from the trees.

Laura Lee tried to catch them.

"It is beautiful here," she said.

She was glad they had come.

Laura Lee had been worried
because Dad might lose his job.

She hoped this trip
would make her feel better.

Dad opened the cabin door.

Laura Lee helped Mom

carry the food cooler inside.

Randy ran in behind them.

"It is so old," said Randy.

"It is nearly dark,"

said Laura Lee.

She looked for a light switch.

But there was no light switch.

"No electricity," said Dad.

Dad lit a lantern.

"It is chilly," said Mom.

"Let's get wood for the stove."

Randy jumped on a bed.

"This is the best place ever,"
he said.

Laura Lee took the room
next to Randy's.

"The sink has no faucet," Mom said.

"How do we get water?"

"There must be a pump outside,"
said Dad.

Laura Lee frowned.

"Where is the bathroom?"
she asked.

Dad pointed to a shed outside.
He smiled.

"It's an outhouse."

Laura Lee shook her head.

"How can we live

without lights and water?"

she asked.

"Or a real bathroom?"

"That is the charm of it," said Dad.

They all went outside.

Dad chopped wood.

Randy stacked it.

Chop, chop sounds filled the air.

Laura Lee and Mom pumped water

into big jars.

"I will light the wood stove,"
said Dad.
"Soon the cabin will be warm."
Laura Lee and Mom
took the jars in.
The cabin was warmer.
"Let's make the beds," said Mom.
Laura Lee's bed was too soft.
She tugged at the sheets.
Then she climbed onto the bed.
She sank into the middle.
"This is too much for me,"
said Laura Lee.

CHAPTER TWO

The whole family
helped make dinner.
"I am hungry," said Randy.
"My stomach is growling,"
Dad agreed.
They all sat down at the table.
Laura Lee bit into a big hamburger.
"That old stove cooks good food,"
she said.
"Food tastes better
in the country," said Dad.
Dad's pan-fried potatoes
were good, too.
After dinner, the family sat
around the wood stove.

The room was warm and cozy.

Laura Lee warmed her toes.

"Are you still worrying about my job, sport?" asked Dad.

"A little," she said. "Aren't you, Dad?"

Dad quoted a Bible verse.

"If you have faith as a mustard seed . . . Nothing will be impossible for you."

"What is faith?" Laura Lee asked.

"Faith is believing that good things will happen," said Dad.

Laura Lee thought about the verse.

Right now, staying at this old cabin for the weekend seemed almost impossible to her.

No water, no electricity.

She would try to have faith.

They roasted marshmallows.

Laura Lee's marshmallow

was hot, sticky, and sweet.

Then Dad told spooky stories.

Laura Lee shivered.

"I'm scared," said Randy.

"It is time for bed," said Mom.

Mom tucked Randy in.

Laura Lee sank into her bed.

She snuggled under the warm quilt.

Telling stories was fun.

Soon she fell fast asleep.

Suddenly there was a crash outside.

Laura Lee jumped.

"It is the ghost of midnight!"

Randy cried.

Mom hugged him.

"It is only an animal," said Dad.

"We will check in the morning."
Laura Lee imagined
a big, black bear
just outside the cabin door.
She covered her head
with the quilt.
"This is too much for me,"
said Laura Lee.

CHAPTER THREE

In the morning,

the whole family went outside.

The cooler was on its side.

It was almost empty.

"Someone took our food," said Mom.

"A food robber!" said Randy.

Laura Lee frowned.

She imagined a big, black bear
robbing their food.

They picked up the food
that was left.

Then they put the cooler in the house.

"Let's go to the store," said Dad.

Everyone climbed into the van.

As they drove, Laura Lee watched
the dark clouds moving
over the mountains.

Some of the clouds looked
like big, black bears.

What if a bear broke into the cabin
while the family was gone?

"It looks like snow," said Mom.

Laura Lee groaned.

"What if we get snowed in?"

Laura Lee asked.

Dad smiled. "I can always take

an extra day off from work."

He stopped the car at the country store.

Everyone went inside.

The air smelled like smoky wood.

Dad pointed.

"A pot-bellied stove," he said.

Laura Lee smiled.

The fat stove

made the room feel nice and cozy.

Mom and Dad shopped.

Laura Lee and Randy

sat at the old counter.

There were big jars
of gumdrops and licorice.
Laura Lee had an ice cream soda.
Randy ate a banana split.
A woman talked with Mom and Dad.
"People here are so friendly,"
said Laura Lee.
When Laura Lee and her family
got back in the car, Laura Lee
was not so worried about bears.

21

As they drove away, there was a noise.

Blam! Hiss!

Dad stopped.

"We have a flat tire," he said.

Mom gave Laura Lee

and Randy some coins.

"Go buy some gumdrops,"

she told them.

"I will help Dad fix the tire."

"What else could go wrong?"
asked Laura Lee.
Then some snowflakes drifted down.
"It is snowing!" said Randy.
"Hooray!"
"This is too much for me,"
said Laura Lee.

CHAPTER FOUR

Laura Lee woke the next morning
to Randy's shouts.
"Snow!" yelled Randy.
"Look at all the snow!"
Laura Lee looked out the window.
Snowflakes danced in the air.
Snow sparkled
on the trees and on the ground.
The bright red cardinal was back.
He flew onto the little pine tree.
The cardinal is hungry,
thought Laura Lee.

Smells of bacon and eggs cooking
made her mouth water.
She put on her slippers
and padded into the kitchen.
Mom spooned a mound of eggs
onto a plate for her.

"Are we snowed in?"

Laura Lee asked.

Dad smiled. "Not yet," he said.

"But getting snowed in

could be fun."

"We could borrow sugar and make

snow ice cream," said Mom.

"We could ski," said Randy.

What if we do get snowed in?

Laura Lee worried.

She remembered Dad's Bible verse.

Why couldn't Laura Lee have faith

as big as a mustard seed?

She would not worry then.

The family put on their ski clothes.

Dad got their skis out of the van.

"The snow looks great," said Dad.

Randy skied away first.

Mom and Dad followed.

Laura Lee slipped and fell.

Dad helped her get up.

They skied toward another cabin
down the road.

The air was fresh and cold.

Laura Lee caught snowflakes
on her tongue.

It was quiet.

A white rabbit ran from the bushes.

"I want to ski down this hill,"
said Randy. "I want to go
all the way to the bottom."
"No," said Dad. "It is too steep."
They stopped at the cabin.
A woman came to the door.
Mom borrowed some sugar.
Dad swept snow from her porch.
"Thanks for the sugar," said Mom.
"Have a nice day," replied the woman.

They skied back toward their cabin.

Laura Lee and Randy fell.

Then Mom and Dad fell, too.

Randy threw a snowball.

Soon the whole family was laughing.

They threw snowballs

until they were white.

"We look like snow ghosts!"

laughed Randy.

Back at their cabin,

Laura Lee saw paw prints

around the garbage can.

"The food robber strikes again!"

Randy cried.

Laura Lee shook her head.

"This is too much for me,"

said Laura Lee.

CHAPTER FIVE

After lunch, Laura Lee and
her family made snow ice cream.
They put sugar and maple syrup
onto fresh snow.
"This tastes good," said Laura Lee.
Then they went outside.
Dad chopped wood.
Laura Lee and Mom tossed birdseed
on the snow.

They put peanut butter
on pieces of tinfoil.
Laura Lee hung the tinfoil on the
little pine tree near her window.
The cardinal came to eat.
A blue jay chased him away.
"Shoo, jay!" Laura Lee cried.
Laura Lee tried to pump water,
but the pump was frozen.
Mom melted snow
for the animals to drink.
Laura Lee had an idea.
She put out scraps of food
on the snow.
She and Randy could hide.
They would see the food robber
come for the food scraps.

"Where is Randy?" Laura Lee asked.

"He was skiing here
a few minutes ago," said Dad.

Laura Lee called.

Randy did not answer.

Laura Lee knocked
on the outhouse door.

Randy was not there.

Laura Lee started to worry.

She imagined a big, black bear
chasing Randy on skis.

"We have to find my brother,"
she said.

Laura Lee and Mom and Dad
put on their skis.

Laura Lee went toward
the neighbor's cabin.

Mom and Dad took other paths.

"Randy is not here,"
said the neighbor.

"I will call the ranger."

Then Laura Lee remembered
the steep hill
Randy wanted to ski down.
Laura Lee's heart
thudded in her chest.
She went to the hill
and started down carefully.
"Randy!" Laura Lee yelled. "Randy!"
What if he is hurt? she thought.
What if he can't hear me?
What if there really is a bear?
Laura Lee thought about
the mustard seed.
I must have faith, she told herself.
Laura Lee prayed silently.
Then she heard a tiny voice.
The voice said, "Help me!"

Laura Lee was scared.

Was Randy trapped somewhere?

Then she saw her brother.

"Laura Lee, help me!" he called.

"My foot is stuck."

Laura Lee skied slowly

to the bottom of the hill.

Randy's foot was stuck

under a tree limb.

She tugged at the limb.

"Oof! It will not budge," she said.

"Mom! Dad! Come quick!"

Laura Lee yelled.

"I found Randy!"

The ranger came first.

Mom and Dad followed.

Together, they lifted the branch

from Randy's leg.

The ranger carried Randy

to his truck.

Mom went with them.

Dad and Laura Lee skied home.

The blue jay scolded

from the little pine tree.

Mom wrapped Randy in a quilt.

Dad made hot chocolate
with marshmallows.

"I am glad you are safe,"
said Laura Lee.

She told Randy about trying to trick
the food robber.

Then she looked out the window.

The food scraps were gone.

"We missed him again?"
asked Randy.

"This is too much for me,"
said Laura Lee.

CHAPTER SIX

The next day, the sun was shining.

The snow began to melt.

Icicles cracked and fell from the roof.

"It is a nice day

for our trip home," said Mom.

Dad and Randy took cans of food

to their neighbor.

Then Dad packed the car.

Laura Lee sat under

the little pine tree.

The blue jay called

from a tall tree nearby.

The cardinal hopped

on the branches of a bush.

Laura Lee made medals
out of tinfoil.

"What are those?" asked Randy.

"I made each of us a medal,"
Laura Lee explained,
"for getting through this weekend."
Mom smiled.

"I thought the food robber
was a big, black bear,"
Laura Lee said.

"I was worried about
getting snowed in.
I was worried about Dad's job."

"Did the mustard seed story help?"
asked Dad.

Laura Lee nodded.

She turned to watch
the cardinal chase the jay.
Laura Lee gave everyone in her
family a medal.
They hung the medals
on the little pine tree.
The cardinal jumped onto a branch.
He pecked at one of the medals.
Laura Lee would miss him.
She would miss the little pine tree, too.

"Everything is packed," said Dad.

"I left peanut butter and bread
on the table," said Mom.

The cabin door was open.

They heard noises from inside.

"Shhh," Mom whispered.

They crept toward the open door.

"A ghost?" said Randy

"A bear?" guessed Laura Lee.

An animal with a white mask
stared back at them from the table.

"A raccoon!" Laura Lee cried.

The raccoon was eating
peanut butter right from the jar.

"That jar was closed," said Mom.

The raccoon ran past them
down the path.
Everyone laughed and laughed.
"This is *much* too much for me,"
said Laura Lee.

THE END

Did you enjoy this book about Laura Lee? I have good news—there are *more* Laura Lee books! Read about them on the following pages.

Don't miss...

Laura Lee and the Monster Sea

There's a monster in the sea... and Laura Lee wants to go home.

Laura Lee and her family are on vacation at the seashore. But Laura Lee is afraid. The waves roar like a monster. Seaweed grabs her feet. Her brother, Randy, chases her with a clam.

With the help of her family, can Laura Lee learn not to be frightened?

Zondervan Publishing House
0-310-59841-9

Don't miss...

Zondervan Publishing House
0-310-59871-0

A Gift from the Sea for Laura Lee

Laura Lee's friend Shona is rich... but Laura Lee is not.

When Laura Lee and her family visit her grandma at the seashore, Laura Lee meets Shona. But Shona says that her family is rich. Will Shona still like Laura Lee even though Laura Lee's family is not rich? Will Laura Lee tell Shona the truth? And who will win the fishing contest?

Laura Lee's dad and grandma help her solve a tough problem in *A Gift from the Sea for Laura Lee*.

Don't miss...

Zondervan Publishing House
0-310-59851-6

A Victory for Laura Lee

**The neighborhood pond
is full of trash...
and Laura Lee is angry.**

When Laura Lee visits the pond
near her house, she finds lots of
trash—and a very sick duck who
is choking on a piece of plastic.
Will the duck live? Can Laura Lee
and her friends clean up the pond
and keep it clean? Can they give
the animals a safe home?